All-of-a-Sudden Susan

All-of-a-Sudden Susan

ELIZABETH COATSWORTH

Illustrated by Richard Cuffari

MACMILLAN PUBLISHING CO., INC.
New York

COLLIER MACMILLAN PUBLISHERS
London

Copyright © 1974 Elizabeth Coatsworth Beston

Copyright © 1974 Macmillan Publishing Co., Inc.

Macmillan Publishing Co., Inc.
866 Third Avenue, New York, N.Y. 10022
Collier-Macmillan Canada Ltd.
Printed in the United States of America

10 9 8 7 6 5 4 3 2 1

Library of Congress Cataloging in Publication Data

Coatsworth, Elizabeth Jane, date
All-of-a-sudden Susan.
[1. Dolls—Fiction.   2. Floods—Fiction]
I. Cuffari, Richard,   date   illus.   II. Title.
PZ7.C6294An   [Fic]   74-6200
ISBN 0-02-722610-7 (lib. bdg.)

For Susan, for whom
this book was written

One

The summer clouds came black and fast like a cavalry charge. The young leaves of the trees were shuddering. Wherever the grass was long, it waved and wavered as if it would run if it could. There were no birds at the feeding stand.

Everything was uneasy, except people, who are always the last to notice what's happening around them.

Joel noticed first.

"Come on, Susan," he said, but stopped to

bounce a last ball into the basket over the garage door. "It's going to rain soon."

"What's a little rain?" asked Susan. "If you're through with that ball, let me have my turn."

"Not on your life," said Joel, who was nearly four years older and didn't take orders from Susan. "Run out to the grape arbor and get Mother and her book moving."

Susan did take orders—sometimes. All of a sudden she saw how black the sky was getting. The sun shone white through the clouds like a frightened moon.

As if a moon could be frightened! thought Susan with disgust. She was a no-nonsense child and she didn't like the funny little feeling she had now. She ran, instead of walking, to the grape arbor where Mrs. Langdon was sitting in an old wicker chair, with her nose in a book "as always," Susan thought.

"Mother!" she called, but her mother didn't

2

hear her at first. Susan had to shake Mrs. Langdon's shoulder before she left the imaginary world in which she had been living and came back to the ordinary, everyday world.

"You startled me, Susan," she protested. "You always speak so suddenly."

Susan didn't stop to argue.

"Joel says to come into the house right away."

"Joel is supposed to do what I say, not the other way around," said Mrs. Langdon with dignity.

"Look!" said Susan. "Feel!"

By now there wasn't any sun at all, and the clouds were racing to cover up the last small patch of blue sky. There was a nasty little wind which humans could now feel as well as trees. It was like a promise of evil things to come. Even Susan's mother, still half in the dream world of her book, felt the threat all about her and got up.

"Perhaps we'll be better off in the house,"

she said as if it had been her own idea. "But there's no need to run, Susan. The rain hasn't begun."

"It will begin any moment," said Susan, coming back to walk beside her mother. She was very fond of her, in fact, though it was like being fond of a person who kept disappearing through a door into another world. "There! I felt the first drop!"

"I didn't feel any," argued Mrs. Langdon, stopping and holding out her hand. A window banged shut above their heads. Joel was closing up the house.

"Come *on*!" said Susan, putting her arm about her mother's waist and pulling her.

"There's no hurry," said Mrs. Langdon and just then the rain did begin to fall in earnest, and covering her book with her scarf to keep the cover from getting spotted, Mrs. Langdon ran up the stairs onto the veranda and into the house.

They had scarcely got inside, when the doorbell rang.

4

"It's the postman!" cried Susan. "Poor post-man! Can't he stay here until this cloudburst is over?"

Mrs. Langdon had already found a chair and her place in her story.

"What?" she said vaguely.

It was no use for Susan to ask again. Her mother's mind was on other things. Susan opened the door and there was the postman, his raincoat and mustache already dripping, holding out half a dozen letters and a long narrow box to Susan.

"The box is for you," he said in his friendly way. "No, I can't come in. It takes more than rain to stop a postman, but thank you just the same."

Two

Susan brought in the letters and handed them to her mother, who slipped them into the back page of her book and went on reading.

"I'll have to tell Father where they are," Susan reminded herself. "Joel! Oh, Joel! Come down! A package has come for me!"

Packages didn't come often to the Langdons, and Joel, after closing the last two or three windows upstairs, came down, cheerful as usual.

7

"I see you got Mother in," he said. "I wonder if she'd have gone right on reading."

"No, of course she wouldn't," said Susan. "She's not an idiot!"

"I wonder sometimes. Anyway, she's in. Wait till I get out my knife. You can't break that string with your fingers."

Susan hated to wait, for as usual Joel took his time, cutting the string as slowly as possible and winding it up on his hand.

"Oh, hurry!" cried Susan, almost snatching her box from his hand.

"Wait a moment! Wait a moment!" said Joel, fending her off. "This is good wrapping paper, too good for you to tear to bits."

Partly Joel believed in saving good paper and string, partly he was teasing Susan a little just because she was always in such a hurry, but he never teased her for long. He handed her the box.

"There you are. It's from Mother's old friend,

Aunt Susan Wendall, whom you're named after."

"She's never sent me anything before," said Susan as she opened the box.

"She's sending you something now," said Joel. "It looks like a doll."

It *was* a doll, but such a doll as neither Joel nor Susan had ever seen before. It was dressed in full skirts and a kerchief and flowered apron, with a white cap on its painted hair and little red leather shoes on its wooden feet. Its stockings were hand-knitted and all its clothes were made of hand-woven cloth. Its wooden arms and legs were jointed at the body and at the knees and elbows, and the wooden face was covered with very soft white kidskin, with glass eyes set in under arching eyebrows, carnation pink cheeks, a fine straight nose, and a rosebud mouth. It was pretty but not in a china doll way. This was a doll with character which looked as if it had always been loved and taken good care of.

"You haven't read the card," Joel reminded Susan.

"Dear Susan," the card ran, in rather old-fashioned writing (for Mrs. Wendall was old enough to be Susan's grandmother and each generation uses a different kind of handwriting). "Emelida has been in my family for nearly two hundred years. Please be good to her. I have no daughter or granddaughter to give her to, so I give her to you as my namesake, with a great deal of love."

"Look, Mother!" cried Susan and Mrs. Langdon put down her book quite quickly for her and examined the doll carefully.

"She even has a little white underbodice with 'E' embroidered on it," Mrs. Langdon said. "Had you noticed, Susan?"

"No, I hadn't," admitted Susan, "but isn't she perfect, Mother? Did you ever see such a doll?"

"Never," said Mrs. Langdon, looking again at the tiny edging of handmade lace along the cap and the black hair under it, painted with such a careful part in the middle. "She's much the oldest and best-taken-care-of doll I have ever seen. We'd better put her in the china closet where she'll be safe."

"No! I want Emelida with me. Aunt Susan sent her to me to love, not to put in the china closet, Mother."

Joel said, "Susan will be careful." He always sided with Susan against anyone else, though not against himself, of course.

In the end Susan went off with Emelida, holding her carefully in her arms.

"She's very brittle," her mother warned, opening her book at the place she had marked with her handkerchief when she closed it. "It would be a pity to break her after all these years," and then Mrs. Langdon forgot Emelida, Susan, and Joel for the imaginary people whose lives went on in such a breath-taking way between the two covers of her book.

"Some people are like that," said Emelida quietly. But only Susan heard her.

Three

As usual when Mr. Langdon came home before dinner, he kissed his wife and then called, "Where's my son, Joel?" He almost never said plain "Joel" but always "My son, Joel," or "My boy, Joel," as if he could never get used to the wonderful fact that he had a son. Nothing that Joel ever did seemed wrong to Mr. Langdon. Actually, he was affectionate to Susan, too, but in an absent-minded way as if she didn't matter very much. He never said "My daughter, Susan," or "My girl, Susan," or called out for her as soon as he entered the house.

"I'm as good as you are, Joel," Susan sometimes said angrily when they were alone, and Joel would just grin.

"You're only a little kid," he'd remind her. "When you get older and prettier, people will pay more attention to you."

He never sympathized with her, but he was nicer to her than most boys are to younger sisters, and sometimes he'd say, half teasing and half out of kindness, "You're my favorite sister, you know."

"I'm your *only* sister," Susan would snap back, but Joel would just rumple her already rumpled hair and say, "You'd still be my favorite if I had a dozen," and it was secretly a great comfort to her to have him say such things, especially after her father had paid her even less attention than usual.

On one of these days when she had been almost ignored, she had decided that she had been adopted.

"Don't talk rot," said Joel when she told him.

"But it explains everything. You look just like the pictures of Father when he was young, but I don't look like Mother or Father either. They thought they wanted a girl, so they adopted me. I guess they made a mistake."

"There you go again!" said Joel. "You know Mother says you look like her sister, Ann."

"And Aunt Ann's dead and who can tell what she looked like from snapshots? No, I'm adopted. I don't care. I like knowing that I'm adopted." But she didn't, and she only half believed it, really.

On the evening of Emelida's arrival, Susan had something important to show her father and for a few minutes he seemed quite interested.

"An old-timer," he said, as he examined her wooden joints. "Not very pretty though."

"No! She's not pretty! She's beautiful!" cried

Susan, but Daddy was lighting a cigarette.

"I didn't know you cared much for dolls," he remarked.

As a matter of fact, Emelida was the first doll Susan had ever cared for. She tagged after Joel too much to think dolls were important. A bicycle or a baseball or a fishing pole were the really important things to Susan. But with the coming of Emelida, all of a sudden Susan knew what it was to love a doll. She loved Emelida. She began to imagine how a dog, a big dog, might catch up Emelida and carry her off. Or a big boy might try to take her to sell to somebody. Or—and Susan went on imagining how, whatever happened, she would come to Emelida's rescue. The dog might bite her, the boy might hit her, but Emelida would be saved.

The next day it was still raining and Susan began to look for a doll's house that Emelida might like to live in. Leaving her on the table or putting her in a bureau drawer wasn't enough for Emelida. She must have a house of her own. Joel suggested fixing up a carton, but that wasn't good enough either. And Susan was too engrossed in her idea to play backgammon or checkers or jacks as they often did on a rainy summer day.

"You're just like Mother," Joel complained. "Perhaps all girls and women have only one idea at a time. Since Emelida came you can think of nothing else."

"I'm not like Mother," Susan fired back. "But I've never had anything of my own that I loved before. Everything nice, like fishing trips, has always gone to 'my son, Joel.' Never to me."

Joel said nothing, but he secretly agreed with her. Now he thought hard.

"I know. There's the little sea chest Great-uncle Samuel had when he was a cabin boy."

"We couldn't get it down the attic stairs."

"You're thinking of the big one with Samuel

Pardee and the American eagle on it. That was the one he had when he was a captain. I mean the little yellow one he used when he was a cabin boy. It isn't heavy. I think Emelida might like it."

It was like Joel to say "Emelida might like it," as if he understood that Emelida was very much of a person whose likes and dislikes were to be considered. Because Joel understood how she felt, Susan followed him without a word up into the attic whose dust and darkness and spiders and strange noises of rain and wind-blown branches scraping across the shingles always scared her. But today she wasn't afraid. Together they carried down the small chest, trying not to bump it on the steps. Susan wiped off the old dust and it looked very nice. It was painted a pumpkin yellow that had scarcely faded at all.

"We'll have to ask Mother if we can use it," said Joel.

As they came into the living room, Mrs. Lang-

19

don looked up and said, "Yes, but be careful of it," and having done her duty, said nothing further.

"We'd better ask Father," Joel said, but Susan couldn't wait.

"Uncle Samuel was Mother's uncle, not Father's," she insisted, and Joel nodded.

From past forgotten dolls, Emelida inherited a doll's bed, a rather too large table, and one chair, which Susan arranged in the bottom of the chest. When she had put a braided pen wiper beside the bed for a rug, she thought the place looked nice. "Now we have to have a door and windows!" she said excitedly. "Can you use Father's little saw?"

"No, I can't," said Joel. "Emelida doesn't need a real door and windows. She's smart enough to imagine them if she wants to."

Susan looked a little doubtful, but when Joel brought his crayons and drew in a door with a knocker and doorknob and added four windows, with white curtains drawn back, she was almost satisfied.

"The windows aren't the same size," she objected, but only halfheartedly.

"They'll look the same size to Emelida. She'll know I meant them to be."

"Yes, I suppose so," said Susan, still a little uncertain.

But she looked down into Emelida's bright dark glass eyes and the eyes stared back at her. For quite a time Susan and Emelida stared into each other's eyes, and slowly Susan realized in a sort of daze that Emelida was magic and could talk and could do anything. Emelida's eyes had hypnotized her.

"Do you like your house, Emelida?" she asked.

"Yes, very much," said Emelida, but once more in a voice only Susan could hear.

Four

Susan's favorite tree was the old apple tree at the bottom of the lawn by the river. In its low branches she loved to sit watching the swallows skimming over the water, or the kingfisher striking down like a falling star, or the occasional small boats going by.

"Emelida would love a tree house," she announced next day, when the rain had stopped.

23

It would be a good deal of work to get the chest, small as it was, down to the apple tree and Joel raised objections.

"Emelida says she wants her house there," Susan said. "She told me so. She's magic, you know."

Joel grinned. His idea that the doll was smart was backfiring, but he had only himself to thank.

"She's just magic for yesterday and today," he stipulated, seeing untold trouble ahead if this idea went on.

"Once you're magic, you're always magic," said Susan serenely.

Very carefully she wrapped Emelida in her own bathrobe so she wouldn't feel any of the bumps of going down the back stairs, and with a good deal of puffing and perspiring and a few complaints from Joel, they got out of the house and into the hot sunshine. It was a day for skipping, but neither of the children had any desire to skip with

24

the sea chest every minute getting heavier and heavier and harder and harder to hold by its rope handles. Getting it up into the tree was the worst part. If Emelida hadn't been magic they could never have done it, and even as it was when they at last succeeded in setting the house on two of the lower branches, one end was up in the air.

Joel propped the lower end higher with a piece of wood he found. Now Susan could sit in a nearby fork and lift the cover and arrange Emelida either in bed or sitting in the chair by the oversized table.

Soon she lifted her out and fitted her on the branch beside her, the doll's wooden knees gripping a twig while her back leaned against another.

"You're safe," said Susan. "How do you like sitting in a tree?'

"I've always liked it very much," said Emelida. "I've sat in dozens in my time. But don't you think the water is very high?"

"Oh, it's often high after a hard rain," said Susan carelessly.

Joel, high up in the top of the tree, asked what Emelida was saying. "You know I can't hear her."

"She just said she always liked climbing trees, and wasn't the water high?"

"It's often like this," said Joel and like Susan he didn't notice just how high it actually was, nor how fast it was running, nor how much trash it was carrying on its current. Both children took the river pretty much for granted.

"Doesn't she ever say anything interesting?" he went on.

"Well, that's interesting to *me*," said Susan. "I didn't know whether she had ever *been* in a tree, even."

"I guess she was born in one. Everything except the kidskin of her face and her big glass eyes is made of wood from some tree or other."

26

"That's not very polite to say when she's listening. Oh, Emelida, I *like* your being a wooden doll. There's magic in wood, in oak trees growing out of acorns that the squirrels have planted, and the lovely gray-stemmed beech trees coming out of little beechnuts."

On his high branch, Joel began to laugh.

"Everything is wonderful! This apple tree grew from an apple pip, and a carrot and a marigold and a sunflower grow from tiny seeds. I guess everything in the world begins small."

"Except you," Susan said. "You've always been my big brother for as far back as I can remember, and you've always known everything."

"At least I know when the lunch bell is ringing, which is more than you seem to know," retorted Joel, climbing down the branches past her. He always knew how to get the best of an argument.

"Shall I bring Emelida?" Susan asked doubtfully. It wasn't easy to get out of an apple tree when one hand is occupied in holding something that mustn't be hurt. She was a little relieved when Joel thought it would be all right to leave Emelida in her house.

"Put the roof down. If it *should* rain again, not a drop will touch her. Stop worrying about her all the time or I'll be sorry you got her."

The fear that Joel might take a dislike to Emelida was enough to make Susan put her down at once on the bed for a nap, closing the lid of the sea chest softly above her. Then she climbed out of the tree and raced Joel to the house and lost the race as she expected to.

"You never give up trying, do you?" Joel teased as they came in. "Some day I wouldn't be surprised if you beat me."

"The paper says we're in for a long rainy spell. We'd better get some food in," Mrs. Langdon said at lunch. "You two come with me and help carry bundles. I mean to buy a lot."

29

"I suppose Noah bought a lot for the ark," suggested Susan.

"Lots of meat for the lions and tigers," said Joel.

"Lots of hay for the horses and cattle," said Susan.

"Lots of milk for the cats," said Mrs. Langdon, joining in the game to everyone's surprise, including her own.

"Lots of seeds for the birds," said Joel.

"Lots of frogs for the snakes," said Susan.

"That's a rather horrid idea," objected Mrs. Langdon, "and I think this game would get horrider and horrider if we went on. We'd better stop."

That was one of the troubles with grown-up people. They'd play along for a little while and then they'd stop when things were just beginning to get interesting.

There was silence for a minute, but Mrs. Langdon broke it.

"I think you'd better bring your raincoats. It was so lovely this morning, but now it's clouding over. And we'll leave dessert until we get back. It will taste all the better by itself in the middle of the afternoon."

Five

Mrs. Langdon was right. They came back in heavy rain, carrying wet paper bags that kept spilling things, with all three of them looking like drowned rats in spite of their raincoats.

"We're just like the Noah family," said Susan as she pushed a soggy bag of groceries onto the kitchen table ."When do you think the animals will begin to come?"

This was turning into a real storm with all the trimmings: rain like a dozen waterfalls, thun-

der in heavy deafening rolls, and lightning terri-
fyingly sharp and stabbing as well as blinding.

"Take off your raincoats," said Mrs. Langdon, hanging hers up in the kitchen to dry, but
Susan started again for the door.

"I can't until I've got Emelida," she said over
her shoulder. But her mother and Joel both
stopped her.

"You can't go out in such a storm," Mrs. Langdon said with more authority than she usually
used.

"Don't be a silly," said Joel, holding Susan's
arm firmly. "The lid of that chest is tight. Nothing's happening to Emelida, but something might
happen to you if you went out in all this lightning.
Look at it! It's lavender. I never saw lavender lightning before."

Susan looked and she was glad to believe that
Joel might be right and that she needn't worry
about Emelida. At least not until later.

33

Then things began to happen fast. Mr. Langdon drove up in the midst of the hullabaloo and left his big car running while he dashed into the house.

"Put on warm coats, all of you, and raincoats too and hats if you have them! I'll get some stuff from the kitchen. The old Red Gully Dam is going to go out, they say, and if it does the lower town will be flooded in half an hour."

"Mercy on us!" cried Mother. "Hurry, children! Where are we supposed to go?"

"There's high land about ten miles out on the highway. Hurry, children!"

Everybody hurried, Mother as fast as anyone. She slammed warm night clothes and everyday clothes and a change of shoes for everyone into a big suitcase which Joel helped her pull bumping down the stairs, across the hall, and then out into the blinding, deafening storm and into the car's trunk. Meanwhile Susan had been helping Father

34

in the kitchen, finding bread and a package of butter and sliced ham and a few cans of meat and fruit. In spite of being all bundled up, she worked very fast and made no false moves. She ended up with two cakes of bitter cooking chocolate. "It will be something to have if we're hungry," she said.

"Good for you!" exclaimed Father. "It's lucky you know how to do things all of a sudden, Susan."

Susan laughed. She was excited and the praise went to her head. She had no clear idea of what it meant when a dam goes out.

"We'd better take something to drink," she said, and with her arms filled with slippery bottles Susan started out for the car. The storm hit her in the face. She was deafened and blinded and one of the bottles slipped out of her clutch and fell, shattering on the walk, but she got the rest onto the floor of the back seat just as Joel came in the door on the other side, after his struggle to help Mother with the suitcase.

"All right, Sis?" he asked. He had never before called her "Sis."

"Fine," she said, on a high note.

The storm exhilarated her. Then she remembered. "Oh! I have to get something," she muttered to nobody in particular and nobody heard her, which was perhaps what she hoped for. In

half a second she had disappeared into the rain. Almost at the same moment Mr. Langdon came out with his arms filled with boxes and bags of food and Joel got out to help him stow them in the trunk. The storm was worse than ever. They could scarcely feel their way along the sides of the car and when Joel got into the back seat, he was too

stupefied to realize that he was alone in it.

Mother had piled a cushion and steamer rugs on the seat with a book or two, "In case we have to sleep in the car," she said. Joel took it for granted that Susan was there, too, beyond the pile of things. He was watching the road, which was filled with cars, all with their lights on, appearing and disappearing like apparitions out of the storm. He knew that his father's glasses were wet and the windshield steamy. Mr. Langdon kept trying to wipe it with the side of one hand.

"Look out! That fool of a car is passing in our lane!" Joel shouted.

Mr. Langdon put on the brakes lightly and skidded only a little. The other car passed by, splashing muddy water all over the Langdons' windshield. The windshield wipers cleared a fan of dirty glass through which Joel peered with his father, muttering what he thought of the driver of the other car. Even Mother was leaning forward trying to see.

"Look out!" she cried once. "A stop sign!"

"You keep looking to the right, Edith," Mr. Langdon said. "Joel and I'll look to the left."

It was terrible driving: blinded as they were, they not only had to look out for other cars, especially those few driving frantically in the other lane going back to the deserted town for something or somebody, but they had to watch every inch of the road for washouts and fallen trees. Several times Mr. Langdon and Joel got out, their heads low between their shoulders, to help others drag a tree out of the way. Once Mr. Langdon got out to tie his handkerchief to a stick which he stuck in the mud to warn others of a gully which stretched halfway across the highway. Everyone in the car was tense, never taking his eyes off the road ahead.

But everything comes to an end. Gradually the rain drove down at them a little less viciously and the thunder and lightning moved away. Gradually the road itself improved, with fewer hazards. They were approaching higher land, out of reach of the river even if it flooded, and the frantic line of cars was slowing a little and there was now no jostling of drivers trying to pass at any cost. Only the few cars in the other lane facing them still drove as if the devil were after them, going back to the empty town for whom? For what? They looked like motorboats at sea, throwing great waves of water to each side as they hurried. But they came less often. It was easier for the windshield wipers to keep the windshield reasonably clear.

Joel sat back, and addressed the corner beyond the steamer rugs and cushion.

"I must say you've kept mighty quiet, Susan," he remarked. "Scared?"

But there was no answer.

"Hey, Susan!" he shouted.

Still there was no answer and all of a sudden Joel realized that Susan wasn't there.

Six

Susan meant to be gone only four or five minutes while she rushed to the apple tree and rescued Emelida. She took it for granted that the others, Joel at least, would notice that she was gone and would wait for her. When she found that her adventure was nothing that could be rushed, she set her teeth and slogged on into the storm anyway. She was never one to give up what she had started to do and in this case Emelida, beautiful Emelida, was waiting for her, sure that she would

41

come. It was hard to pick her way, but the lightning helped. Joel was right. It *is* lavender, she thought as a bolt veined the sky, and a crash told her that it had struck nearby.

"I'm not afraid," said Susan out loud. "I'm not afraid." But the wind and the rain whipped the words out of her mouth, as if she hadn't spoken.

"I'm coming, Emelida!" she called and perhaps there are now faint echoes of her words a thousand miles away where the storm carried them. Half a dozen times she fell on the rain-wet, slippery meadow grass, but she was always up again in a second. She couldn't see her way, but she knew it was downhill. When she got to the orchard, the water was almost up to her knees. She felt her way from tree to tree, with the water always getting a little deeper.

Something far back in her mind said coldly and calmly, "Don't be a fool. Get back to the car while you can," but Susan wouldn't listen. She drowned out the voice of reason, and the voice of love shouted, out loud, "I'm coming, Emelida! Don't be afraid!"

Did Emelida answer her? Susan heard no sound, but all of a sudden she moved with a new certainty, splashing among the apple trees. It was as if a life line had been thrown to her and she had it in her hand and only needed to follow it to find Emelida. She was not surprised when she bumped into a broad trunk, and reaching up, felt the sea chest which had once belonged to a bold little boy who ran away to sea.

"I'm here," she reassured Emelida. "I'll have you out and under my raincoat in half a jiffy," and she began to climb into the low branches as she spoke.

Did she hear a small clear voice answer, "I'm not so sure of that, my dear"?

It was on the third attempt that Susan got herself and her heavy coat and raincoat and her rain-soaked shoes and water-logged socks up into the fork of the apple tree and sat there panting. She no longer noticed the lightning and thunder much. It was almost as if they had been crashing and flaring at her for half her life, but she still had to bend low to fight the force of the wind and the rain which seemed bent on tearing her out of the tree. She was just leaning forward to pry open the top of the chest with one hand while holding herself in place with her other hand gripping a branch, when she heard a different sound and turned to hang onto the branch with both hands. It was a horrible sound and she knew instinctively, although she had never heard it before, that it meant death and desolation. It was the sound of a wall of water rushing down their little river like an avalanche.

"The dam's gone out," the inner voice re-marked reasonably, but the everyday Susan screamed twice before her mouth was filled with water. She felt the tree lurch under her, hold by its long, strong roots for a minute, and then give way and go hurrying down this new and terrible river. As the tree gave way, it found its equilibrium even in this turmoil. Susan's face came out of the water. She was still clinging to the apple tree, in fact wedged into the crotch of branches more firmly than ever. And the sea chest, too, had been wedged between the branches where Joel had fitted it. But it wouldn't remain there long. They were part now of the great, noisy, cluttered rolling rush of water. It's faster than sliding down a steep hill on a sled, Susan thought.

Who was it who said, so faintly that she scarcely heard it, "This is fun"? Susan hoped it was Emelida who had spoken. A doll might say a thing like that, but a girl who had lost her family and the house where she had been born, and who in all probability would soon be drowned, would be a fool to think this was fun, especially a girl who had not only herself but Emelida to look after.

Well, there was nothing she could do for anybody now except wait to see what would happen next, but she must get Emelida out of her doll's house before it was carried away. Already the door and windows with their white curtains were half obliterated by the water, and the house, or sea

chest, whichever way she thought of it, was stirring uneasily, moving back and forth among its branches like a horse eager to be up and away.

And just then as she was thinking of horses, a dead horse went by, a terrible sight especially to eyes which might look like the horse's eyes before long. More and more dead animals went by and a few that were alive and still swimming, although now there seemed no shore to which they could swim.

Poor, poor things, thought Susan. Oh, I *wish* I could help you!

She forgot even Emelida for a moment as something caught in the branches of her tree. It was a white rooster that had been riding on a tilting crate. It pecked weakly at Susan's hands as she lifted it off and put it up as high as she could reach among the leaves.

"Stay still," she told it. "You're as safe as I am now, though I don't know that that means much."

It was a few moments later that she succeeded in getting the sea chest open. Emelida had fallen out of bed onto the floor, but she seemed all right.

"I'm sorry. I'm afraid that you'll get wet," she told Emelida as she lifted her out and put her under her raincoat.

"I'm not made of sugar. I won't melt," Emelida answered cheerfully, her voice rather muffled by the raincoat.

Seven

The next couple of hours were frightful and yet they had a certain excitement to them. Susan's spirits rose to meet the danger. She was tense as a fiddle string, frightened and yet almost happy. She wasn't alone. Emelida didn't speak often, but when she did, her voice was that small sweet voice that Susan had first heard, though still somewhat muffled by the raincoat.

"Can you breathe?" Susan asked once anxiously.

50

"Dolls can always breathe," said Emelida, adding a little sharply, "What did you think when you shut me up in the little sea chest?"

"I didn't know then that you were alive the way people are alive."

"Well, I was. Just as much as I am now."

A little later she exclaimed somewhat shrilly, "Look out for that house!"

Susan hadn't seen the house coming, and of course Emelida couldn't have seen it from under the raincoat if she hadn't been magic. It was a small house, going round and round as it came down the river. Sometimes it seemed to stick on the bottom and then it would lurch to a halt, with the water clawing high up one side. Then when Susan was breathing more easily, it would start forward again, coming straight after the apple tree as if it were pursuing it.

All the time more broken things were hurrying by, chairs and tables, wooden beds, animals.

Susan reached out to catch a little dog, but when at last with a great effort she pulled it to the apple tree, she saw that it was dead.

"Too bad," said Emelida sadly. "Let it go. The river will bury it."

"Why didn't you tell me it was dead before I nearly fell out of the tree trying to rescue it?" Susan demanded with some indignation.

"You didn't ask me," said Emelida smugly.

Just then the house did bump into their apple tree, which went under for a moment, scaring Susan, and then bobbed up alongside of the house, having spilled the little sea chest.

But Susan and Emelida and the rooster emerged still in the tree, though streaming wet, and Susan at least was spitting out water. She hadn't had time to be frightened when she heard Emelida's small voice under her raincoat staying, "Do you see the kitten in the window? *She's* alive."

Susan looked at the house rocking past them,

and there indeed was a marmalade kitten clinging to the sill of the nearest window, its nails dug into the wood.

"It's as safe there as it would be with us," said Susan, but Emelida knew better.

"No, the house is breaking up. It won't last long."

Susan liked cats, what she knew of them, for they hadn't a cat of their own. But from trying to save the little dog she knew how hard it was to pull something into the tree and this cat looked as if it would hold on to the windowsill for dear life.

"You can do it," said Emelida softly.

It was not raining so hard now, and the claps of thunder and the splintering lightning had moved off into the distance. Susan slid a little farther out along her bough, still holding tightly to the branch overhead. Once she heard her raincoat tear as it caught on a twig. Bother! Mother won't like that!

Susan thought, and then she thought very clearly, If I'm dead, she won't care about a raincoat.

The house stopped again with a jerk and Susan's tree scraped along its side. Susan had one glimpse of the bedroom furniture floating and bumping inside, and then she leaned across a third bough and caught at the cat with both hands. To her surprise, it let go of the windowsill and twisting about, caught hold of her arm with all its claws.

It's lucky I have a heavy coat on under this raincoat, Susan thought. I can feel the tips of its claws even now.

Aloud she said soothingly, "Kitty, kitty, poor kitty, you're all right now."

"That's as may be," said Emelida. "Kitten! Behave yourself, or she'll throw you into the river!"

The kitten seemed to understand. Slowly and fearfully it allowed itself to let go and at last curled in Susan's lap, a wet, bedraggled creature in a wet, bedraggled lap.

"There's a boat,
It's afloat!"

sang the little voice against Susan's chest, and Susan, looking out eagerly, saw a rowboat higher up the river. There were three people in it, not rowing but fending off debris with their oars. Two of them seemed to be men and the third was a woman. They saw her and the woman waved.

They called to her, but she couldn't make out their words in all the rush of water and the hub-bub of the still falling rain.

"They said they couldn't take you in," said Emelida. "They're overloaded now. But they'll tell the first rescue boat."

"A lot of good that will do," grumbled Susan. She was feeling very, very tired now, and although it was a warm day, she was shivering.

"This is an adventure you'll tell your grand-children about," said Emelida.

"I probably won't have any grandchildren," snapped Susan.

"Hoity! Toity!" said Emelida.

It was as near to a quarrel as they ever came.

Eight

The rain was lessening, the thunderstorm had passed down the river and almost out of sight and hearing, but still the river tore on, overflowing its banks, carrying away new trees and boathouses and houses, too, and every sort of debris. Once Susan saw a dead woman. Her body was snagged in an eddy among a grove of flooded willows. For a moment Susan saw her face and was surprised at how much like any woman's face it looked.

Susan couldn't do anything, but it was a solemn moment and she knew she might be next. The tree gave a lurch as some of the branches snarled in one of the willows, still standing. Then it went on again, spinning.

Although she was rather dizzy, Susan repeated the Lord's Prayer out loud. It was the only way she could think of to tell the dead woman how sorry she was.

Halfway through, Emelida's little voice joined in.

"Very proper," said Emelida after the "amen." "Probably there have been other drowned people going by, but we haven't noticed them in all the debris. Goodness gracious! There's a grandfather's clock and it's bowing to us!"

That made Susan laugh, as Emelida perhaps intended she should. Behind her in its tangle of branches, the rooster made a little clucking sound as if he wanted some attention and Susan turned and patted him gently on his feathery back. He may have been a pet bird, for under Susan's hand he made another more contented sound, and then Susan turned to pat the yellow kitten shivering in her lap. Probably her hand made the kitten begin to feel that it was safe, for it gave a short anxious purr.

"I don't know what will happen to any of us," Susan told them, "but the same thing will happen to us all. I'll take care of you as long as I can."

"Well said," remarked Emelida approvingly. "I really think you're a very nice child, as nice as any I've ever known. But it's no time for compliments. You'll never ride downriver in a flood again. You'd better enjoy it."

"Enjoy it?" cried Susan, surprised and rather indignant.

"I said, 'Enjoy it,'" repeated Emelida. "I told you before, it is fun."

"With that poor dead woman and all?" Susan demanded.

"You can't keep people from dying," said Emelida. "They do it all the time and we may be doing it, too, for all we know. But meantime, enjoy yourself."

Susan didn't reply, but soon she found that she was feeling a little different. She became more and more a part of the river's excitement.

The river, usually so humdrum and quiet, had changed into quite another river, a rushing, roaring, swirling, eddying creature, fierce and merry, reaching out to seize anything it could and then tumbling it upside down or right side up, losing it in an eddy along the bank, and then pouncing to seize it again, and carrying it off with a triumphant swish. It was like riding a tiger to ride this river, but so far the apple tree with its many branches and many roots was riding it like an outrigger canoe.

In her new mood Susan patted the branch nearest her.

"Good for you!" she cried and now she had stopped being afraid. What was going to happen would happen, but meantime she had this wild ride, the brave apple tree, the river beside itself with elemental joy and violence, Emelida against her chest and the rooster and the kitten in their places. She felt like Noah in his ark, she was like a Viking in a dragon ship, she was like Columbus in the little *Santa Maria*—oh, there had been a thousand voyagers on just such perilous waters as she now sailed!

"I wish I had a pennant for the good ship *Apple Tree*," she told Emelida.

"Use your red scarf," said Emelida. "It's nearly dry and will flutter, which may be a rather good idea anyway."

"I'm not asking for help, if that's what you mean," said Susan indignantly. "I'm just putting up a pennant. You were the one who told me I should enjoy the voyage."

"So I did, so I did," said Emelida. "But it's well to keep an eye on both aspects of this journey."

It may have been the red scarf which caught the eye of the elderly man sitting astride the roof-tree of a bungalow at the edge of the river. It was surrounded by water, but its foundations must have been good for it was still standing though the veranda had been torn off and was hanging to it by one edge. He saw Susan and took a big handkerchief out of his coat pocket and waved, but it was a worried wave and his face looked worried, worried not about himself but about Susan and the apple tree.

"We're all right!" she called to him, waving her own handkerchief. "We'll send help for you soon!"

He didn't hear what she said, but he looked

a little more cheerful as if he realized that at least she wasn't frightened. It was nice to see another living human being, and to have someone to wave to. And the old man wasn't the last person Susan

saw. Clinging to the dormer of another house there were two people, a man and a woman, and Susan waved and shouted to them and they waved back. The woman was crying, which Susan thought was silly of her.

"She's probably wet and cold," Susan told Emelida, "but they're perfectly safe. There's nothing to cry about."

"Some people like to cry," said Emelida, from two hundred years of experience.

"I'd probably be crying now if it weren't for you," admitted Susan and the idea made her laugh. She wished Joel were along so that he could share the glory of the flood, and thinking of glory made her start singing, "Glory! Glory! Hallelujah!" at the top of her lungs, "As we go marching on!"

Nine

It was in this happy mood that the rescue launch found her and rescued her—and at her insistence the rooster and the kitten—from the apple tree, as well, of course, as Emelida.

"Weren't you scared?" asked the policeman who was handling the launch. "That apple tree was mighty tippy."

"That was part of the fun," said Susan.

"Punch drunk," said the other officer in a low voice.

"Is your name Langdon?" asked the first policeman. "A pretty worried family is waiting for you, if that's your name."

Susan's face fell. She could imagine what they'd all say to her. She was in for the scolding of her life.

"Yes," was all she answered.

Later, the launch was crowded with people and with a dog that had to be kept away from Susan's marmalade kitten and the rooster. Most people would have thought the launch ride was as much excitement as they wanted, dodging obstructions and even with the engine at low speed tearing down the river, with great wings of water curling back on either side of the prow.

But to Susan it didn't seem very interesting after her apple tree, which had grounded again but would soon be lurching along behind them, she knew.

The thought of her family sobered her. They'd

all scold her, especially her father. Her shoulders hunched and her mouth drooped, knowing what was coming. Of course she deserved it, running away like that without even letting anyone know.

"You did it to save me," whispered a very small voice which only she could hear. It made her feel better and she braced herself for the ordeal ahead.

But when she reached the curve of the river where the launch was able to land, and where waited a big group of people who had friends or relatives still somewhere up the river, nothing happened as she had thought. She was handed over the side of the boat to the soggy shore, with the kitten under one arm and the rooster under the other. She wasn't an easy person to hug, but she was being hugged all the same, hugged by Father and by Mother and by Joel, all at once and separately. If they had ever been angry at her, there had been time for anger to burn away in the

fire of their anxiety. Now they felt only joy.

"Look out! Be careful of Emelida!" Susan cried and Joel unbuttoned her raincoat and took Emelida out, her clothes a little rumpled, but her pink mouth smiling as ever.

"I had to go back to save her," said Susan.

"Oh, Susan!" Mother said and Father took the rooster and Mother took the marmalade kitten, and as they turned away, Susan gave a last look at the crazy river and there, sure enough, was the S.S. *Apple Tree* with her red scarf still flying.

Susan waved.

"That was our vessel," she said. "I was captain."

"Darling!" Mother cried again. "Uncle Samuel would be proud to have you in the family, Susan."

"You're my brave girl," said Father in just the tone he used to Joel, but if anything even warmer.

And all of a sudden Susan knew, once and for

all, that she really mattered a great deal to everyone.

"I could have told you so from the beginning,
but you wouldn't have believed me," said Emelida.

Only Susan heard her, for of course Emelida
was magic.

ELIZABETH COATSWORTH first made her mark as a poet; and poetry, by her own statement, remains her real calling. Her first volume of poems, *Fox Footprints,* was published in 1923.

The author of more than sixty books for young readers, Miss Coatsworth is considered one of the truly distinguished writers for children of this century. In 1931 she won the Newbery Award for *The Cat Who Went to Heaven,* and in 1968 she was honored as runner-up for the Hans Christian Andersen Award, the only international award given an author for his complete work.